SUPERMAN ATTACK OF THE TOYMAN

BY **JOHN SAZAKLIS**
WITH **JOHN FARLEY**
ILLUSTRATED BY **ANDY SMITH**

SUPERMAN created by Jerry Siegel and Joe Shuster

HARPER FESTIVAL
An Imprint of HarperCollinsPublishers

HarperFestival is an imprint of HarperCollins Publishers.

Superman: Attack of the Toyman
Copyright © 2012 DC Comics.
SUPERMAN and all related characters and elements are trademarks of and © DC Comics.
(s12)

HARP2593
Manufactured in China.

Library of Congress catalog card number: 2011945727
ISBN 978-0-06-188535-8
Book design by John Sazaklis
12 13 14 15 16 SCP 10 9 8 7 6 5 4 3 2 1
❖
First Edition

SUPERMAN

Sent to Earth from Krypton, Superman was raised as Clark Kent by farmers in Smallville, Kansas, and taught to value truth and justice. When not saving the world, Clark is a mild-mannered reporter for Metropolis's newspaper the *Daily Planet*.

LOIS LANE

Lois is also a journalist for the *Daily Planet* newspaper. She won an award for her scoop about being saved by the mysterious hero of Metropolis and naming him "Superman." She competes with Clark Kent to get exclusive stories on the Man of Steel. Little does she know that both men are one and the same.

JIMMY OLSEN

Young Jimmy is an excellent photographer as well as a budding journalist. He works with Clark and Lois at the *Daily Planet* and is often pulled into exciting adventures with the news team as they chronicle the daring deeds of Superman.

THE TOYMAN

Winslow Schott is a toy maker and brilliant inventor. He once owned a successful store that sold old-fashioned toys. Then large media companies created digital devices that made his quaint toys obsolete and put his store out of business. Poor and angry, Mr. Schott vowed revenge and transformed into the Toyman.

All across the city, the good citizens of Metropolis are asleep in their beds. Beware! Winslow Schott, the mad toy maker, is up way past his bedtime.

Mr. Schott has fashioned a new series of tiny remote-control cars that carry explosives. He will send them to the companies that shut down his toy store.

"In order to succeed in business," muses the madman, "you have to blow away the competition!"

Lois, Clark, and Jimmy arrive at the Daily Planet Building. Without warning, a deafening explosion rocks the block. KA-BOOM!

"What was that?" Jimmy asks. Before anyone can answer, there are two more explosions.

KA-BOOM! KA-BOOM! Smoke billows up between the buildings and debris litters the streets.

"I'll tell you what that is," Lois replies. "It's our front-page story. Let's go!" The daring reporter pulls the young photographer into the chaos.
"Mr. Kent, are you coming?" Jimmy asks his friend.
"You two go on," Clark says. "I'll go get help!"

Once his friends are out of sight, Clark changes into his alter ego. "This looks like a job for Superman!" he says.

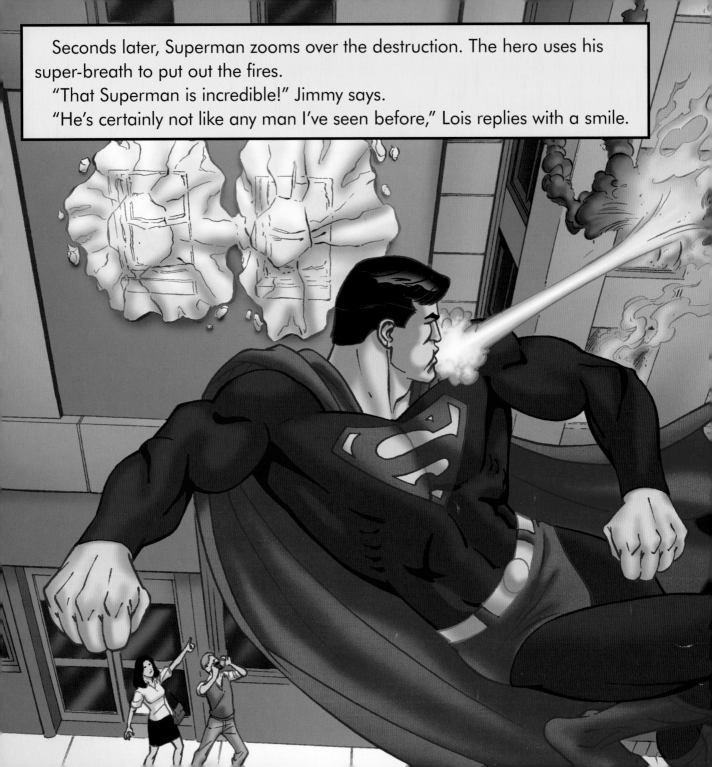

Seconds later, Superman zooms over the destruction. The hero uses his super-breath to put out the fires.

"That Superman is incredible!" Jimmy says.

"He's certainly not like any man I've seen before," Lois replies with a smile.

"He's nothing!" yells an angry voice. The startled reporters turn around. They see a colorful character holding a small electronic device in his hand.

"Who are you?" Lois yells back.

"I *was* a lowly toy maker, now I *am* the TOYMAN!"

The Toyman guides one of his remote-control cars into the Daily Planet Building. In a blinding flash, the main lobby blows out toward the journalists. FWOOM!

Superman rushes to the rescue . . . but he's too late! Lois crawls out of the wreckage and falls into Superman's arms.

"Jimmy . . ." She gasps. "He's . . . he's trapped!"

The Man of Steel glares at his new foe. He is furious.

The Toyman quickly grabs another one of his inventions. It is a rocket-powered pogo stick.

"Gotta bounce!" He sneers and propels himself into the sky. Superman lets the villain escape; he must save his friend first.

With lightning speed, the Man of Steel uses his super-strength and lifts the heavy rubble off of Jimmy. Then he carries the rattled reporters to a nearby ambulance for medical treatment.

"Hey, Superman, I recognize those remote-control cars," Jimmy whispers. "I had one when I was a kid. I got it at Winslow's World."

Lois's eyes light up. "Winslow's World was an old toy store forced out of business by the new wave of digital gadgets. We wrote a story about the poor owner, Mr. Schott. Could that be him?"

"Clearly he's upset about how his life turned out. That's no excuse to hurt people. It's time to teach the Toyman the error of his ways," says Superman. Then he speeds off.

On the other side of town, the terrible Toyman returns to his hideout. The base of operations is his old toy shop, Winslow's World.

"That caped clod is sure to find me here," he says to his toys. "But we'll be ready for him."

Superman smashes through the roof. "Playtime is over!" he says.

"Actually, the fun has just begun!" shouts the Toyman.

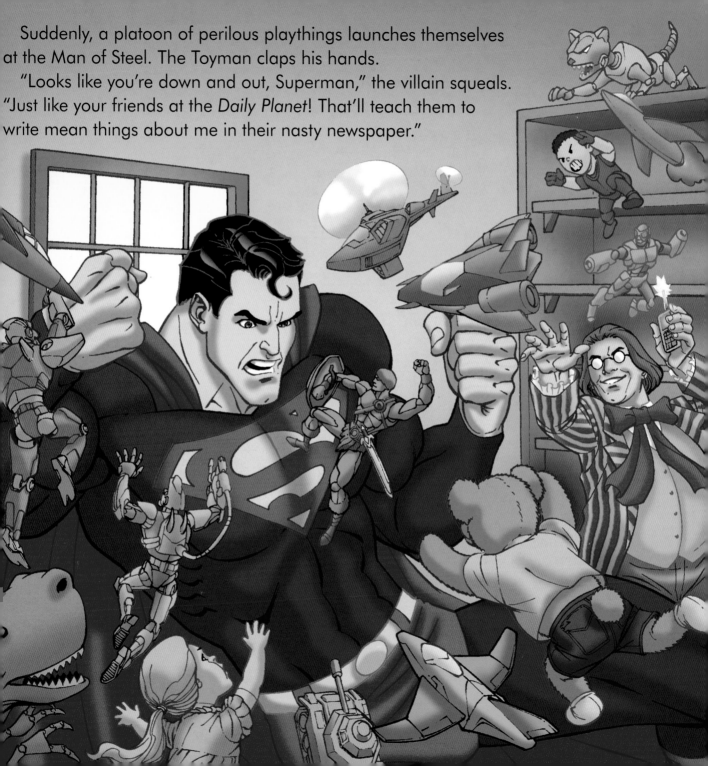

Suddenly, a platoon of perilous playthings launches themselves at the Man of Steel. The Toyman claps his hands.

"Looks like you're down and out, Superman," the villain squeals. "Just like your friends at the *Daily Planet*! That'll teach them to write mean things about me in their nasty newspaper."

Superman punches his way through the onslaught of toys. For every one he sends smashing into a wall, another two spring up to replace it. The Toyman laughs harder as the Man of Steel continues his struggle against this endless attack.

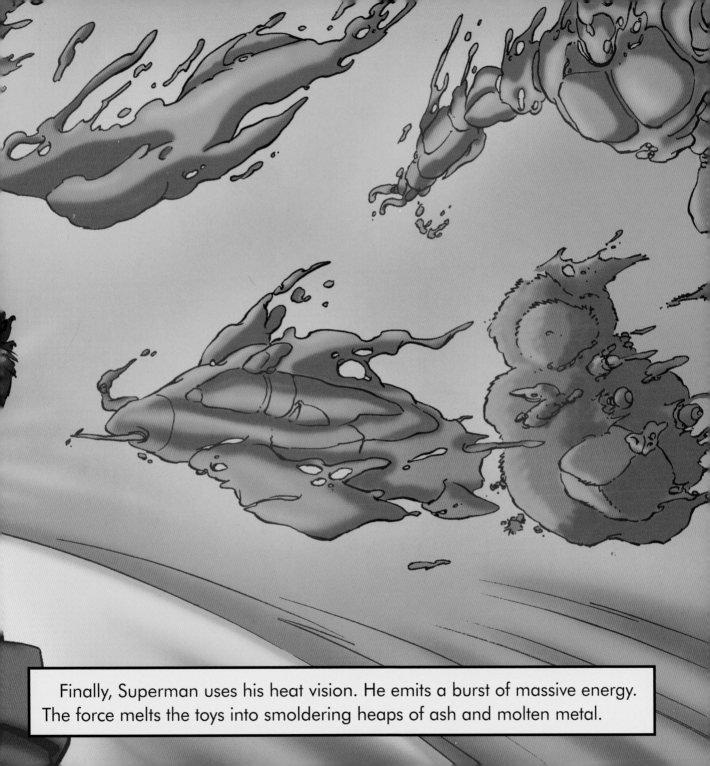

Finally, Superman uses his heat vision. He emits a burst of massive energy. The force melts the toys into smoldering heaps of ash and molten metal.

Superman picks up a remaining tank and crunches it into a ball.

"I believe in recycling trash," Superman says. "Now it's your turn, Toyman."

The scared scoundrel spins around and scurries to the exit.

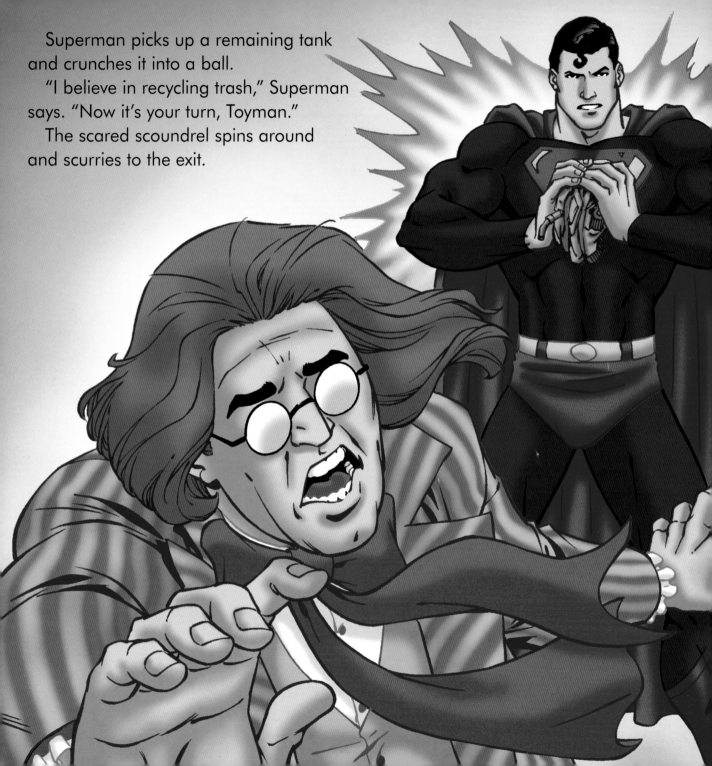

Before he can escape, Toyman finds his path blocked by Lois and Jimmy.
"Not so fast, Mr. Schott," says Lois.
"We have a score to settle," adds Jimmy.
"Fine by me," yells the Toyman. "I never play fair!"

The insane inventor pulls out a peashooter and takes aim.
He blows two pellets filled with sleeping gas at the reporters.
Superman swoops in to save them. With his super-breath,
he sends the pellets back at the Toyman.

WHOOSH! They pop open in front of the villain's face.

"You big blue bully!" the Toyman yells at Superman as he breathes the gas. Then the foe tumbles to the ground and falls asleep.

"Too bad, Toyman," says Lois. "Too bad."

"Looks like cranky little Winslow just needed a nap." Jimmy laughs.

"Thanks to your timely arrival, Toyman is no longer a menace to Metropolis," Superman tells them. His super-hearing picks up the sound of police cars far in the distance. "My work here is done," he says, and flies away through the hole in the roof.

Seconds later, Clark Kent walks in with two officers.
"Where have you been, Clark?" Lois cries.
"I told you I was going to get help," Clark says, and points to the policemen.
"Better late than never," grumbles Lois.

After padlocking the abandoned toy shop, the policemen carry the dozing evildoer to their squad car.

"Gosh, Mr. Kent," Jimmy says. "You missed all the excitement!"

"I just can't keep up with you two daredevils." Clark chuckles.

"Welcome to the big city, farm boy," Lois says.

Together, the news team rushes to the Daily Planet Building. Their trouble with the Toyman will certainly make a great story!